To Mary and family with love,

The Other Side of the Fence

Story by Jean Marie Rose Wojtas, SJ

S. Jean Marie Wojtas, sj

Illustrations by Eric Le Mire

Published by Crooked Tree Stories of Ada, Michigan.
Direct inquiries to Betty Epperly at www.crookedtreestories.com

This book is dedicated to my family, who lost their home in Grand Rapids, Michigan, during the Great Depression in the 1930s. Hastily, my parents purchased a small thirteen-acre farm in eastern Ottawa County. My parents and older brothers and sisters worked diligently to create a home out of a shack and to build a productive farm from the acreage. I am grateful to my parents, Carl and Lottie Wojtas and my brothers and sisters: Eugene, Caroline, Theresa, Paul, Harry, and my youngest brother Tom.

Our parents, Carl and Lottie Wojtas, circa 1945

One might think that just because
a child grows up on a farm,
that liking cows comes naturally -
'cause how can they bring any harm?

But just as special and unique
as meadow flowers grow,
so does a cow's personality
develop from head to toe.

First in line came Bessie,
a huge and stately cow;
a milk-producing Holstein
whose glare said, "Milk us NOW!"

Second came a Guernsey cow
with "harmless horns" they said.
She walked behind the leader,
this gentle cow named Red.

Thirdly came another cow,
whose nature was spiteful and hatin'-
bawling, kicking, and jumping fences;
my brothers named her Satan.

Last in line clumped Danny the Bull,
a young pigeon-toed steer.
He took his time, curiously looking behind -
a carefree caboose at the rear.

Day after day, I watched this parade
from the other side of the fence;
only to see within each cow's eyes
a deep distrust, I could sense.

"You need another chore," Pa said,
"my small Sparrow, my dear.
Those cows need water twice a day.
You'll do it. Do you hear?"

At these words a panic struck -
I couldn't say a word.
I dared not question Pa's command;
his words were clearly heard.

Water those monsters? I'll surely be killed.
I shivered with fear and dread.
What could I do? I felt so small.
While a stampede raced in my head.

My mother understood and said,
"My child, don't dismay.
Just fill the trough with water
when the cows are far away."

My job went along successfully.
I watered them well each day,
watching to see that the cows were far off -
a task I didn't delay.

But then one sunny summer day,
something else went wrong!
Another task was added -
my job list grew quite long.

"Tomorrow, when it's time for milking,
YOU'LL bring back those cows!
You're big enough to get them," said Pa.
"Just move them along and don't browse."

"Oh, no," I thought, "the FEAR again!"
I shivered and my heart sank.
"Drive those beasts all by myself? How?"
My mind went blank.

"Don't be frightened," my brother said,
as he voiced my worry aloud.
"I'll show you how to call the cows,
your MOOING will make you proud."

"Cup your hands around your mouth
and imitate their bellow.
Call 'em from here, outside this fence
and don't be quite so mellow."

I practiced all evening, I bellowed and mooed -
I worked with all my might.
My lungs expanded, my face turned red.
I got the sound just right!

Then finally the time had come,
my performance was at hand.
How would those cows respond
to a new voice of command?

Way off in the distance,
the far pasture I could see;
the cows with their heads down,
grazed contentedly.

So, I went to work on MOOING
as loud as I could.
Outside of the fence,
I suspensefully stood.

Now just as sure as the evening sun
settles into the night,
the cows looked up and turned around -
what a breathtaking sight!

I did it! I did it!
I can breathe once again.
I stayed on the outside,
and brought those beasts right in!

The procession continued swiftly,
they all walked in a row:
Bessie, Red, Satan, and Dan,
their order would always show.

Suddenly, they were all gathered up
close beside the gate.
Was Pa coming to let them through?
How long could they patiently wait?

It was time to get my father.
My new task was all done!
Pleasing him, surprising him
and impressing him would be fun.

I wanted him to notice
that I had done my chore.
But all he did was look at me
and ask me to do more…

"Drop down the gate," he said to me,
"and let the cows go through.
I'll signal you from inside the barn
with a loud yoo-hoo."

Oh, no one to help me
get out of this mess.
Surely to my father
I'll have to confess:

"I CAN'T DO THIS!"

I slowed down my pace,
to give myself time
to think of a plan,
with some reason or rhyme.

When I passed the ol' outhouse
and noticed how near,
a new plan of action
became crystal clear.

I prepared the escape
by wedging the door -
wide enough to get me through,
and not an inch more.

"If I drop the gate logs
in the opposite way,
the cows will have to wait.
There will be a delay."

So I went straight to work,
even though I was scared,
when a make-believe courage
within me flared.

I dropped down the bottom log!
Then came the middle!
Down crashed the top log,
exposing me - a child so little.

Into the outhouse
I zoomed out of sight,
a race with the cows -
"I WON! All RIGHT!"

I did it! My heart raced,
as the cows passed on by;
no fence between us,
and I did NOT die!

Now the lessons I learned
from the story I told
are not only about cows,
but my secrets untold.

The fear of my pa
caused a very high fence
to grow right between us
at my own expense.

The fear of the truth
worried my soul.
Would my pa still like me
if I were not bold?

But the truth of the matter
is that Pa really DID know
of my fear of the cows.
My courage DID show.

For later that evening
as we went off to bed,

I overheard the proud words
that my father said:

"GUESS WHAT, MA!"

"Rosie dropped the gate down
and let those critters through,
even though she was afraid.
Today, her courage grew."

At his words, I smiled and sighed
while drifting off to sleep.
Pa's words meant so much to me -
a treasure I'll always keep.

The End

Although Danny the Bull always followed last,
he was a friend to my brothers, faithful and steadfast.

Made in the USA
Lexington, KY
08 June 2019